The Tale of the Talking Face

The Tale of the Talking Face

WRITTEN AND ILLUSTRATED BY

K. G. SUBRAMANYAN

NEW YORK LONDON CALCUTTA

Seagull Books 2011

First published by Seagull Books in 1998

Text and Illustrations © K. G. Subramanyan 1998

ISBN-13   978 0 8574 2 005 3

British Library Cataloguing-in-Publication Data

A catalogue record for this book is available from the British Library

Printed and bound by Hyam Enterprises, Calcutta, India

The TALe oF The talking FACE

There was an old country.
And it had a king.
He was a good and kind king.
But he died as all kings do
when they grow old and weak.

But he died with a heavy heart.
He felt he had not done enough
for his people.
The land was dry and stony,
not lush and green.
People were lean and hungry,
not gay and well-fed.
I have a long way to go,
he wrote in his diary,
the day before he died.

But when kings die they do not
go very far.
Their bodies go to the funeral pyre
and the ashes go into a river or sea.
They go no further.

The whole country wept.
Tears come quickly to people
who are poor and sad.
They come quicker when they lose
somebody they like.

But there were some in the king's court
whose tears were not real.
They wore them on their eyes
like icing on the cake.

They were not sorry he died
for they wanted badly
to be king themselves.
They had lived near him and
watched him do his things,
walk, talk, hold court and rule the land.
What he could do they felt they
could do as well.

So while the king watched the poor land
and grew lean and old,
they watched him on the throne
and grew round and fat.

When the mourning was over
and the flags went up the poles,
they all rushed to the throne
knocking each other down.
But the throne was too small
for any one of them.
Other thrones had to be made
designed to their sizes.

So they rushed to the throne makers.
The throne makers said,
The thrones take a long time to make.
There are lots of things to do to make a throne—
choose a tree, fell it, saw it,
turn it, put it together and, lastly,
get it blessed.
And for each you have to find the days
when the stars are good.
That took a long, long time.

But the throne that is cannot be kept empty

for a very long time.

So they chose the young princess

to put on the throne.

For just a short while, they said,

till the new throne came.

The princess was small and frail

and when she sat back on the throne

her feet rose off the ground.

Which the courtiers grinned to see.

They ran in the meantime to get

the new throne made.

Large enough, they said,

For the future king.

Which each one thought he was.

For this they knew the British were

the best in the world.

They had kept their kingship going

just to keep this trade alive.

And they alone of all knew how
to make large thrones.
Large enough to hold Albert and Victoria
side by side.

For a while the little princess
can play in the present one.
And she will not do this for long.
She would be more interested in
rolling her curls than ruling her country.
And would lay aside the sceptre
for the powder-puff.
So they had nothing to fear.

But this princess was no such princess.
She did not dream
of dresses and ribbons
or curlers and cosmetics.
She had grown up in the lap
of a father who had visions
of doing people good.
And she wanted to do good too.

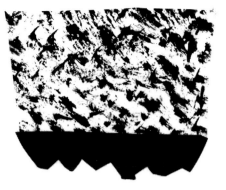

Harder than he did.
As you will see soon enough.

One fine morning the princess
walked into her garden.
The sun fell on the earth
like a wrap of gold;
the green leaves
shone like gems;
the roses nodded
and blushed;
and the jasmines
flashed their teeth.
Butterflies flew here and there
with huge flapping wings
inlaid with brilliant colours.
The wind blew against them
and put them in a flutter
and they swayed and steered around
with awkward pleasure.

But a butterfly's pleasure is hard for a
princess to read.
She felt they were struggling.
That brought tears to her eyes.
Poor little things! she said, Where did they get
these gaudy over-sized wings?
Surely in some cheap ready-made store?
How they make them reel!
How can they sit
on the tiny tips of flowers?

Someone had to help them out.
And who was there but her?
So she ran to her room
and came back with her
nail-clipping scissors.
She caught a butterfly
and clipped her wings short,
rounding each wing with care.

Then she threw her into the air
as high as she could.
But down the butterfly
shivered to the ground.

This perplexed the princess.
With puckered eyebrows she pondered.
I have left too much wing, she thought.

Then she picked up the butterfly
and clipped more of her wings,
leaving just two tiny stubs.
And she threw her into the air
even higher than before.

But down the butterfly came
wriggling with pain.

This irritated the princess.
Here I lighten her wings,
but she is too lazy to fly! she cried,
You could rip the heads
off little fools such as she!

She left her struggling in the grass.
And reached out to help the others.

But the others were wiser.
They had quickly steered away.

The princess went home in anger.
It was not easy to do good to people.
They were all a silly lot.
You had to force things down their throats.

In the big palace there was
a dark corner under the stairs,
where hung the picture of a face.
Her father, the late king, had once told her
that it talked to him
when he went near it.
And wisely, too.

Old papa is crazy,
she had thought at the time,
Old people tend to be.

But now that she was on the throne,
she would do what others did.
So she walked up to it
and the face tilted and smiled.
Be sure to be good
before you do anyone good, my dear, it said.
Be sure to love people before you
go to their help.
Or they will get hurt.
And will hurt you too.

The princess was not pleased.
Love was not a word the princess understood,
love of the old-fashioned kind.
It was through such love
That her papa came to grief.

And, besides, pictures cannot be prophets.

So she covered it with a mirror.
Where she could see her own beaming face.

The mirror-face had magic.
She smirked, she smiled, put out her tongue
and pulled her eyes open,
then broke into a peal of laughter.
She could be anything she wanted.

The princess grew by leaps and bounds
once she sat on the throne.
Not that her bones grew larger
or her muscles added weight.
She did not wait for that.

She had things made for herself,
bodies and limbs, heads and masks,
vests and visors,
like you see in suits of armour.
Not to fit her wee body
but to rig it out larger than life.
Arms that started at the shoulders
and went further than the fingertips.
Legs that were as tall as stilts.

Over-sized busts, some flat and pious
with strings of beads,
some full and heavy with gold and pearls.
Then masks and trappings,
some bland and severe,
some gilded and enamelled.

Eyes that winked and ogled,
or saw you with a sneer,
or looked daggers at you,
or froze you with a stare.
And mouths that whispered soft
or blared out like trumpets.

Rigged in these she filled the throne
quicker than people thought.
She is quite an eyeful,
like the great queens of history, they said.
She moves like a minaret, some declared.
She rolls like a giant wave, others remarked.

This filled her with a sense of power.
And she wheeled into action quick.
By royal order she closed the ports.
No throne could be brought in now.

And she opened court.
Not with those fuddy-duddies
who had worn out the eyes of people
with their fat bodies and fatuous smiles
but strapping young men and women.
Some not so young
but groomed and brushed so to seem.

She pinned to the chest of each
a large iron medal,
Which they were flattered with.
And gave them each an iron belt to wear.
Which they wore with pride.
To each chair in court
she fixed a large magnet.
And she herself wore strong magnets
with her bracelets and rings.

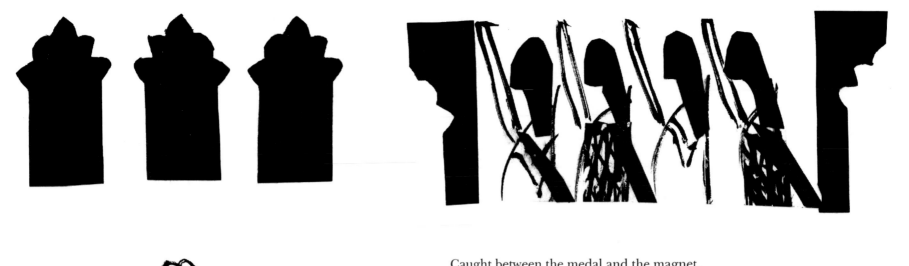

Caught between the medal and the magnet,
the courtiers behaved as she wanted.
They sat when she wanted,
they rose when she wanted.
They bowed or waved,
marched or gestured at her bidding.
They talked or kept mum
at the snap of her fingers.

There was order in the court.
They all sat in a row like letters in a book.
They walked in a row
like the rings of a centipede.
And they felt mighty pleased.

For once they did not have to think!
For once they did not have to take decisions!
For once they felt like babes
in a mother's arms!

She is our mother, they all said.
She is everything to us.
She is our land, our life.
She is our hope and salvation.

The belly of the princess rose with pleasure
when she heard all this.
My naughty little, nasty little children,
she said to herself.
And treated them as such.

The old fatties did not have a chance.
She had already paved their door fronts
with banana peels.
So when they stepped out,
plop they slipped and fell.

That was hard on their rolls of flesh.
It was hard too on their over-strained hearts.
So they chose to sit on their balconies
and weep.

The princess was now all set
to do good to her people.
The people were poor.
The people were weak.
The land was arid.
She had to change it all.
She couldn't bear to rule
over a barren land like this.

But before she did all that
she needed to know her people,
she had to see the land.
She heard that people are easy to know
when they are down and out.
So she went to them
when they were in distress.
Troubled by flood or fire.
Or stricken by drought or famine.

And never empty-handed.
She took them tiny bags of flour
and tiny little blankets.
Marked with her coat of arms.

The people were pleased no end.
Our tiny little godmother, they said.
We may have lost our village
but we have a pretty bag of flour!
We may be naked now,
but with the blanket on the wall
we will hardly be noticed!

They wanted to embrace and kiss her.
She gave her wooden leg
to the men to embrace.
She gave her wooden cheeks
to the women to kiss.
She sat on her wooden haunches
on their clay-washed floor
and sipped with wooden lips
their watery soup.

This pleased them more.
She may not be like us
but she does things like us,
they exclaimed
with great delight.

Then she screwed on her whistle-voice
and talked to them.
All your troubles are there because
you do not have a voice, she said,
The right kind of voice.
And the world seems a poor place
because you don't see it in proper light.
I shall change all this.

She gave to each a whistle
and with it a printed score.
Blow them and feel happy, she said,
with a pat on the back.
Then she gave them each
a pair of green glasses.
Wear them and see the world,
she said with a disarming smile.

They put their lips to the whistle and blew,
following the printed score.
They all blew, Long live the princess.
Then they blew, Poverty is dead.
Then they blew, The green age is here.
Then, The princess is us.
If she is well, we are well.

In the shrill note of the whistle,
all these sounded real and true.
And their pulse beat faster.
They felt their breath fill their bellies
more roundly than bread ever did.

The louder the noise, the greater their happiness.

Then they wore the glasses.
Good gracious! they all gasped.
Whatever they saw was green.
The bare fields were green,
the brown rocks were green.
The blue sky was green.
They had never seen
so much green before.

Just imagine! they said,
We slogged all our lives
to make the country green,
and it was as simple as that!

The princess was really smart.
Those whistles and green glasses
had brought about a revolution.

Now, said the princess,
Poor though we are,
We have our own kind of power—word power.
Word power has always
helped us in the past.

Our medicine-men cured aches and pains
with words, our magicians put demons to
flight with words.
What can other things do
that words cannot? she asked.

Nothing! cried the people.
They had come to see
what power they truly had.

Then she said, Our land may be old
but a little brushing up
can make it as good as new.

Sure it can! everyone agreed.

The princess was pleased.
Let us spruce up our country,
she declared.
Like a sick man feels better
when he is sponged and dressed,
a sick country feels better when it
starts looking smart.
And besides, we have to be smart
before other people.
The tourists and the diplomats,
who come with their cameras and cinema kits,
peeping out of car windows
and peering down from helicopters.

Today a country has no secrets
unless it knows how to keep them,
she said darkly.

Smart girl, that princess.
She had sold them the idea.
Let us start from near the roads, she said,
That is where the visitors pass.

They grew flowering hedges
on the sides of the roads.
They tilled the land behind,
three fields deep, and grew rice,
maize and mustard from special
imported seeds.
They sprayed them with white manure.
They dusted them with pesticides.
They bred birds and beasts
from glade to glade.
Peacock, bulbul and long-tailed parakeet.
Nilgai, tiger and spotted antelope.

FESTIVAL 3

We shall now hold festivals,
said the princess.
Yes, festivals, agreed the people.

Dressed in gay old finery
they hopped and danced.
Maybe bony under their billowing clothes.
Maybe sad under their smiles.

But festivals were fun,
for the people who watched.
Bony is Beautiful! Sadness is Sweet,
cried the tourist posters.
The tourists agreed.
All this was so rare
in their part of the world.

We have to keep the show going,
the princess continued,
We of the great third world!
The great third world!
The people wondered.

SADNESS IS SWEET

Bony is beautiful

In their native tongues the
third world meant heaven.
The first was the world just here
and the second world the one below.
Is ours really heaven?
they asked themselves with pride.

The show went on.

In cities and towns
the princess ordered flags and buntings
to fly from rooftops,
sequinned curtains
to hang from windows.
She planted blinking neon signs
at all the street corners.
She lined the roads with hoardings
to mask the murky shadows.

But the village houses were hard to mask.
They had sordid entrances
and filthy backyards.

They had ragged roofs.
The only things that were clean
were their two side-walls.

The princess asked her architects to help.
Your challenge, gentlemen, she said.
The architects gathered and discussed
and held seminars.
This challenge was no challenge.
They came up with a plan.

All walls should be side-walls, their report ran,
and this is easy to achieve.
Where will the doors and windows be?
the people asked in panic.
On the roof, they said.
How can that be? asked the people in doubt.

It can, if you have the courage.
Like rats have,
when they dig their holes from the top.
Or the moles for that matter.
Or the wiggly earthworm.

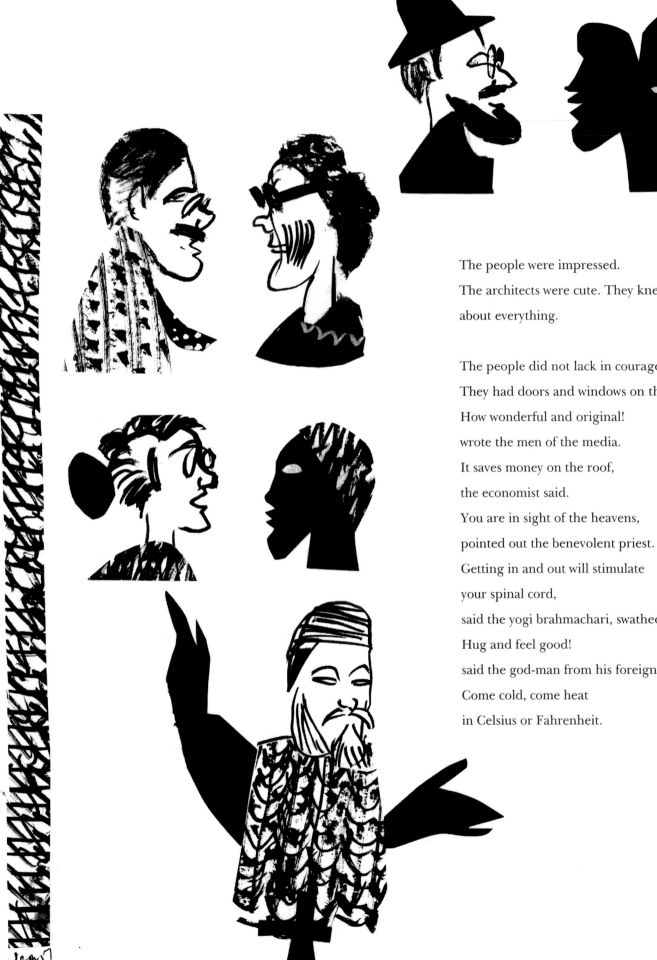

The people were impressed.
The architects were cute. They knew all
about everything.

The people did not lack in courage.
They had doors and windows on the roof.
How wonderful and original!
wrote the men of the media.
It saves money on the roof,
the economist said.
You are in sight of the heavens,
pointed out the benevolent priest.
Getting in and out will stimulate
your spinal cord,
said the yogi brahmachari, swathed in silk.
Hug and feel good!
said the god-man from his foreign retreat,
Come cold, come heat
in Celsius or Fahrenheit.

Amongst all this the people felt better.
When the artists stencilled
the princess' visage on all the blank walls,
in blue, yellow and pink,
they felt royal, indeed.

Except when the sun beat down
on their heads,
or the rain filled their rooms,
or the dust lay heavy
on whatever there was.
That was messy, indeed.

The princess saw solutions for all this
if the people would wait.
And they know how to wait,
she told herself with a sigh.

But there she went wrong.
The people were not the same any more.
And they were too many.
Things were scarce. Life was hard.
All was topsy-turvy.
There weren't even enough whistles
and goggles to go round.

So they came to see the world as it was
with their naked eyes,
the brown barren land
a few steps from the roadside shows.

And without the whistles in their mouth
they got back their voices too
So they howled in grief and anger.

Is this all that has come to be,
from these five-year leaps? they groaned.

They meant the five-year plans.
The princess got that from her
father who was a number five fan.

She loved the five-year cycle
for reasons of her own.
It took you rushing forward
without the pain of looking back.
And by the time you ended
you forgot what you sought.
Even lost the count
of what you gained or lost.

You planned things in the first year.

You fanned your hopes in the next.

You discussed them in the third.

You detailed them in the fourth.

Then canned the whole thing in the fifth.

And the cycle started again.

What came to be came to be.

The country went on its path.

And the chariot of power rolled on.

People could bear it no longer.

They felt they were being taken for a ride.

The princess had lost her old magic

As they were now open-eyed.

To hell with this! cried the people.

And this cry spread far and wide.

Then they ran amok.

They pulled down the buntings and billboards.

They battered the arbours and fountains.

They looted the markets and stores.

And fouled up the flowerbeds.

No! No! warned the princess,
now ageing to be queen.

Her hair had greyed at the corners.
Her eyes were shadowed with worry.
And her mouth was sewed up with wrinkles.

But stamping her foot she swore
that she can't let this be,
such crass rapacity.

Then she sat with her inner council
and came to the point straight.
I have shown them my smile,
I have shown them my guile.
Now I shall show them my claws instead.

Sure, sure, the council said.

Those who won't see reason
will be hauled up for treason, she rhymed.

Sure, sure, the council chimed.

So she sent for her redress squad.

They were trained to dress the nation's wounds
and mend its rents and tears.
They patted the hares
and pampered the hounds
and took them unawares.

She sent them to the people.
Do a smooth job, she said.
They sealed the mouths of many.
And bandaged their burning eyes
with yards and yards of tape.
Scented jasmine, rose and sandal
to suit their separate tastes.

The queen is generous, they said,
To friend and foe alike.

Then they played to them her message.

Just for a short while, friends.
The wind of progress is blowing.
Please rest your eyes and throats.
Plug up your ears and banish your fears.
When the wind has blown us rich
the bands will fall apart.

And show you a transformed land
brimming with wealth and cheer.
Then you can shout to your heart's content
in square after square.

Time passed
and there was no change.

Only vacant talk and waiting.
People went raving mad.
Their eyes' anguish and throats' stifled rage
broke out of their bodies like guns.

They hardly knew what they were doing.
Their anger was mindless and blind.
They never saw where they were going.
Or what they left behind.

They shot at each other.
They fought with the state.
They tried to blow up the palace
and disturb the court.

They even sniped at the queen.

That sent her into shivers.

She went running to her mirror.
Then stopped short in dismay.
Good lord! What did she see there?
Hair that had yellowed like hay,
and a face harrowed with fear.

So she went behind to the picture
and asked it in tearful shame.
Where, oh where, have I gone astray?

Everywhere, said the face.

A nation is people, my dear.
People with heads and hearts,
People with hopes and dreams.
You had to help them to help themselves.
Help them to love the land.
Help them to love each other.

Then they would have built

the land themselves

in the image of their hearts.

Singing as they toiled, beaming as they bled,

swinging through all the trouble,

braving all obstacles.

It would have cost you nothing.

But you treated people like playthings.

You hardly let them free.

They slaved to serve your wishes.

And your endless vanity.

I only wanted their good, wailed the queen.

Sadly so, my dear.

But you didn't know what it was.

You strapped them to the wheel of progress,

and knocked them into bags of bones.

Is there no way out now?

the queen asked in desperation.

Can I not make amends?

You surely can, the face said,
fixing its amused eye on her.

Just walk out of your costume.
Break out of your pride.
And go straight to their homesteads.
Tell them they are free.
Tell them the land is theirs,
they can turn it into arcady.
And tell them you will work with them,
even follow their lead.
Then, even if they mauled you in anger
you'd have given them what they need.

Which is, the right to love their land.
The right to remake it themselves.

She shuddered at the thought.

She did not have the courage
to put aside the costume
and all that came with it.

Nor would her friends allow her.
No, never, they all cried.
This is what we know you by.
Don't heed the picture's prattle,
it will leave you high and dry.

Then the queen's secretary sailed in
and whispered in her ear,
Tomorrow, Your Majesty,
the Media Kings are here.
To make a film on you,
on the story of your success,
your heroes and your gods,
and how you keep your flag flying
against such hopeless odds.

You have asked them all to come at nine
and wait at the lotus pond.

All right, she sighed, it's another day.
Then she asked the lady, By the way,
are all things set, for safety?

Sure, Your Majesty.

Landmines under the lilies.
Sten guns in the shade.
Frogmen in the tanks and ponds
and guardsmen at the gates.

That sounded safe enough.

So early the next morning,
sharp at five to nine
the queen walked out to meet these men,
in the merciless sunshine.

Rigged out in her regalia
and proud as queens should be,
with measured step and chin drawn up
in royal dignity.

Then it happened all of a sudden.

She stumbled on a lily.
A landmine burst underfoot.
And blew her into bits.

There amidst the ruins of her costume
and all her equipage
lay a blank, bewildered girl
streaked blue and brown with age.

The courtiers jumped and shouted,
We will avenge our Queen!
They ran berserk, losing their heads
and left ten thousand dead.

Then the whole procession
to the royal palace came,
and decided amongst themselves
that the picture was to blame.

So they tore the picture to pieces
and threw these overhead.
But when they flew in the wind they panicked
that its magic may still spread.

And pasted them back though not so exact
into an image of sorts;
the ears were shapeless,
the eyes were weird;
while the nose and chin were still intact,
the mouth had disappeared.

A face from Francis Bacon!
some said. Oh, no! An icon,
said others with a nod.
Eyeless, earless, mouthless,
he is as harmless now as God.

Better this way, the wise declared,
In this vile and vicious world.

No evil will he see or hear
nor ever speak a word.

That makes him worship-worthy;
so go down on your knees.
Sing sacred hymns and observe fasts;
hold anniversaries.

For while you sing you can do your thing,
without any guilt or fear,
if you raise him high against the sky,
the world is wholly yours.

Now no more bars to hold seminars,
and play marbles with his words;
or send afloat in the reachless air
gas balloons and birds.